Oscar
got the blame.

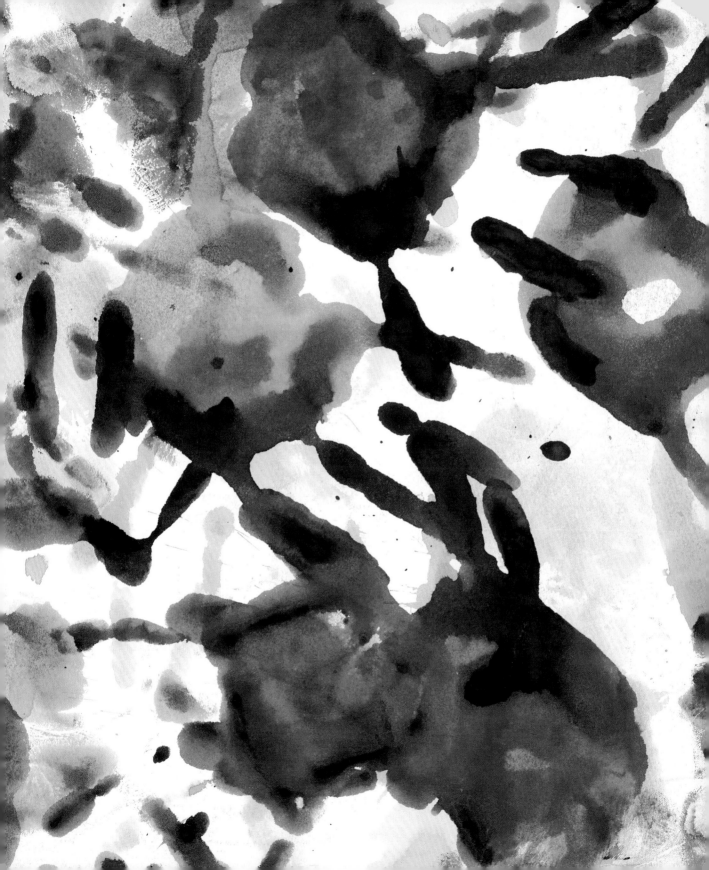

Oscar
got the blame.

Tony Ross

Red Fox

To Katy,
and her invisible friend Mandy,
who made the endpapers of this book
out of a clean piece of paper

A Red Fox Book

Published by Random House Children's Books

20 Vauxhall Bridge Road, London SW1V 2SA

A division of Random House UK Ltd

London Melbourne Sydney Auckland

Johannesburg and agencies throughout the world

First published in 1987 by Andersen Press

Beaver edition 1989

Reprinted 1989

Red Fox edition 1995

9 10 8

© 1987 by Tony Ross

Printed in China

RANDOM HOUSE UK Limited Reg. No. 954009

ISBN 0 09 957280 X

This is Oscar . . .

. . . and this is Oscar's friend, Billy.
Oscar's mum and dad think Oscar made Billy up.

Whenever Oscar talked about Billy, his mum and dad said,
"Don't be silly."

But Oscar and Billy were the best of friends . . .

. . . day and night.

Sometimes, Oscar let Billy have some of his dinner ...

. . . but then had to eat it all himself.

When Billy left little bits of mud around the house . . .

. . . Oscar got the blame.

When Billy dressed the dog in Dad's things . . .

. . . Oscar got the blame.

When Billy put frogs in Granny's slippers . . .

. . . Oscar got the blame.

When Billy made breakfast . . .

. . . Oscar got the blame.

When Billy washed the cat . . .

. . . Oscar got the blame.

And when Billy left the bathroom taps running...

. . . Oscar got the blame

. . . and was sent to bed without a story.

"It's not fair!" said Oscar.
"Nobody believes in my friend Billy."

"THEY NEVER DO!" said Billy.

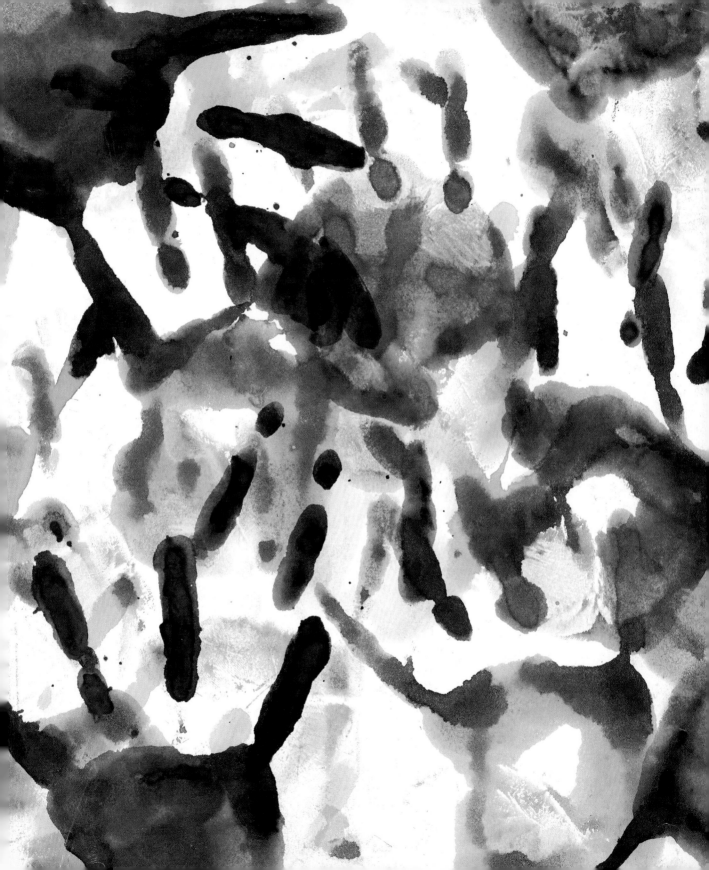

Some bestselling Red Fox picture books